THE PENGUIN POETS

SUNRISE

Frederick Seidel was born in St. Louis in 1936 and attended
Harvard University. He was Paris editor of the *Paris Review*
and currently serves as an advisory editor. Mr. Seidel has
taught English at Rutgers University and now lives in New
York City.

Sunrise is the 1979 Lamont Poetry Selection of the Academy of American poets.

From 1954 through 1974 the Lamont Poetry Selection supported the publication and distribution of twenty first books of poems. Since 1975 this distinguished award has been given for an American poet's second book. The judges for 1979 were William Harmon, Maxine Kumin, and Charles Wright.

SUNRISE

Poems by

FREDERICK SEIDEL

Penguin Books

Penguin Books Ltd, Harmondsworth,
Middlesex, England
Penguin Books, 625 Madison Avenue,
New York, New York 10022, U.S.A.
Penguin Books Australia Ltd, Ringwood,
Victoria, Australia
Penguin Books Canada Limited, 2801 John Street,
Markham, Ontario, Canada L3R 1B4
Penguin Books (N.Z.) Ltd, 182–190 Wairau Road,
Auckland 10, New Zealand

First published in the United States of America in
simultaneous hardcover and paperback editions by
The Viking Press and Penguin Books 1980

LIBRARY OF CONGRESS CATALOGING IN PUBLICATION DATA
Seidel, Frederick, 1936–
Sunrise.
(The Penguin poets)
I. Title.
[PS3569.E5S8 1980] 811'.54 79-25519
ISBN 0 14 042.280 3

Printed in the United States of America by
American Book–Stratford Press, Inc., Saddle Brook, New Jersey
Set in V.I.P. Bembo

Some of these poems have previously appeared in *The American Literary Anthology 3,* edited by George Plimpton and Peter Ardery; *American Poetry Review; Harvard Advocate; The Listener* (London); *New American Review; The New York Review of Books; Partisan Review; Poetry;* and *Poets on Street Corners,* edited by Olga Carlisle.

To Jill Fox

and to Clare and Bernardo Bertolucci

Contents

SUNRISE

1968

A football spirals through the oyster glow
Of dawn dope and fog in L.A.'s
Bel Air, punted perfectly. The foot
That punted it is absolutely stoned.

A rising starlet leans her head against the tire
Of a replica Cord,
A bonfire of red hair out of
Focus in the fog. Serenading her,
A boy plucks "God Bless America" from a guitar.
Vascular spasm has made the boy's hands blue
Even after hours of opium.

Fifty or so of the original
Four hundred
At the fundraiser,
Robert Kennedy for President, the remnants, lie
Exposed as snails around the swimming pool, stretched
Out on the paths, and in the gardens, and the drive.
Many dreams their famous bodies have filled.

The host, a rock superstar, has
A huge cake of opium,
Which he refers to as "King Kong,"
And which he serves on a silver salver
Under a glass bell to his close friends,
So called,
Which means all mankind apparently,
Except the fuzz,

1

Sticky as tar, the color of coffee,
A quarter of a million dollars going up in smoke.

This is Paradise painted
On the inside of an eggshell
With the light outside showing through,
Subtropical trees and flowers and lawns,
Clammy as albumen in the fog,
And smelling of fog. Backlit
And diffuse, the murdered
Voityck Frokowski, Abigail Folger and Sharon Tate
Sit together without faces.

This is the future.
Their future is the future. The future
Has been born,
The present is the afterbirth,
These bloodshot and blue acres of flowerbeds and stars.
Robert Kennedy will be killed.
It is '68, the campaign year—
And the beginning of a new day.

People are waiting.
When the chauffeur–bodyguard arrives
For work and walks
Into the ballroom, now recording studio, herds
Of breasts turn round, it seems in silence,
Like cattle turning to face a sound.
Like cattle lined up to face the dawn.

Shining eyes seeing all or nothing,
In the silence.

A stranger, and wearing a suit,
Has to be John the Baptist,
At least, come
To say someone else is coming.
He hikes up his shoulder holster
Self-consciously, meeting their gaze.
That is as sensitive as the future gets.

Death Valley

Antonioni walks in the desert shooting
Zabriskie Point. He does not perspire
Because it is dry. His twill trousers stay pressed,
He wears desert boots and a viewfinder,
He has a profile he could shave with, sharp
And meek, like the eyesight of the deaf,
With which he is trying to find America,
A pick for prospecting passive as a dowser.
He has followed his nose into the desert.

Crew and cast mush over the burning lake
Shivering and floaty like a mirage.
The light makes it hard to see. Four million dollars
And cameras ripple over the alkali
Waiting for the director to breathe on them.
How even and epic his wingbeats are for a small fellow.
He sips cigarette after cigarette
And turns in Italian to consult his English
Girlfriend and screenwriter, who is beautiful.

In Arizona only the saguaros
And everybody else were taller than he was.
Selah. He draws in the gypsum dust selah
He squats on his heels for the love scene, finally
The technicians are spray-dyeing the dust darker.
It looks unreal, but it will dry lighter,
Puffs of quadroon smoke back out of the spray guns.
The Open Theater are naked and made up.
Between his name and néant are his eyes.

The Trip

Nothing is human or alien at this altitude,
Almost a drug high, one mile in the blue,
I am flying over what I will have to live through:
So this is love, four curving jet trails of flock.
How different it was to look up and see
The train you rode on curving away from you
On a long bend—like your child body, part
Of you, apart from you. It felt so odd,
How hauntingly it straightened and disappeared.

This is love reflected in the window
Tippling a complimentary cup of broth,
Myself and Magritte, the desert takes a drink.
I gaze through my forehead at the rising desert,
Dots and dashes like meanings, pain-points of green,
Cactus crucifying the beautiful emptiness.
I hold my own hand while I slowly find
The horizon on the other side of my eyes.
It I feel close to, it cannot come near:

There and beyond one like heaven, as Che is. Once,
On the new Metroliner fleeing New York,
Fleeing the same girl I am flying to . . .
The experimental train dreamed of flight,
Eupeptic sleek plastic, Muzak, its steel skin twinkled.
We rose on music from under Park Avenue
To the fourth floors of Harlem where only the bricked-up
Windows didn't reflect us. I saw them, the slightly
Lighter bricks within the brick window frames.

The Room and the Cloud

The tan table of the desert is an empty
Sunlit plaza by de Chirico
That has no meaning, that is like the desert
Rising in the windows of an Astrojet
As it so coldly dips to right itself.
A rich man in Arizona drives a tan
Mercedes, bulbous and weightless as an astronaut.
It barely moves, it walks through space the way Mao does,
Tan freezing silence like a freeze frame.

Across a desk top, in his fuselage,
The rudimentary tail brain of his two
Propels the largest living dinosaur,
Schizophrenia. And when he tilts
His head Tucson turns, a slow veronica,
The horizon lifts to one side like a drawbridge.
Years float by, cold Novocaine nirvana
Aloft in a holding pattern as if forever.
They bring the stairs up, First Class ducks out first.

Step one is to be rich. The two men are beaming:
My host with the Mercedes and his guest
Fly in on the freeway through a desert noon.
Their conversation seems to them an oasis,
Air conditioning sanitizes the air.
The giant saguaros stand up, without hearts or hair,
Autoplastic adaption that can't fail.
I see a desert. I look down at the typed page:
We are the room and the cloud on its painted ceiling.

The Soul Mate

Your eyes gazed
Sparkling and dark as hooves,
They had seen you through languor and error.
They were so still. They were a child.
They were wet like hours
And hours of cold rain.

Sixty-seven flesh inches
Utterly removed, of spirit
For the sake of nobody,
That one could love but not know—
Like death if you are God.
So close to me, my soul mate, like a projection.

I'd loved you gliding through St. Paul's sniffing
The torch of yellow flowers,
The torch had not lit the way.
Winter flowers, yourself a flame
In winter. In the cold
Like a moth in a flame.

I seemed to speak,
I seemed never to stop.
You tossed your head back and a cloud
Of hair from your eyes,
You listened with the beautiful
Waiting look of someone

Waiting to be introduced,
Without wings but without weight, oh light!
As the fist which has learned how
Waving goodbye, opening and closing up to the air
To breathe. The child
Stares past his hand. The blank stares at the child.

Goodbye.

Sunrise

For Blair Fox

The gold watch that retired free will was constant dawn.
Constant sunrise. But then it was dawn. Christ rose,
White-faced gold bulging the horizon
Like too much honey in a spoon, an instant
Stretching forever that would not spill; constant
Sunrise blocked by the buildings opposite;
Constant sunrise before it was light. Then it
Was dawn. A shoe shined dully like liquorice.
A hand flowed toward the silent clock radio.

Bicentennial April, the two hundredth
Lash of the revolving lighthouse wink,
Spread out on the ceiling like a groundcloth.
Whole dream: *a child stood up.* Dream 2: *yearning,*
Supine, head downhill on a hill. Dream: *turning*
And turning, a swan patrols his empty nest,
Loops of an eighteenth-century signature, swan crest,
Mother and cygnet have been devoured by the dogs.
The dogs the dogs. *A shadow shivered with leaves.*

Perth, Denpasar, Djakarta, Bangkok, Bom
Bombom bay. Dogs are man's greatest invention. Dogs.
They were nice dogs. Find a bottle of Dom
Pérignon in Western Australia.
Find life on Mars. Find Jesus. "You are a failya,"
The President of the United States said.
He was killed, and she became Bob's. His head,
Robert Kennedy's, lay as if removed
In the lap of a Puerto Rican boy praying.

9

Ladies and Gentlemen, the President
Of the United States, fall in the air,
A dim streetlight past dawn not living to repent,
Ghostwalks by the canal, the blood still dry
Inside soaked street shoes, hands washed clean that try
To cup the rain that ends the drought. No one
Spoke. Blindfolds, plus the huge curtains had been drawn.
Because of his back he had to be on his back.
Neither woman dreamed a friend was the other.

Innocence. Water particles and rainbow
Above the sweet smell of gasoline—hiss of a hose
Drumming the suds off the town car's whitewalls, which glow!
Pink-soled gum boots, pink gums of the ebony chauffeur,
Pink summer evenings of strontium 90, remember?
Vestal black panther tar stills the street.
The coolness of the enormous lawns. Repeat.
O innocent water particles and rainbow
Above the sweet smell of gas, hiss of the hose!

When you are little, a knee of your knickers torn,
The freshness of rain about to fall is what
It would be like not to have been born.
Believe. Believed they were lined up to take showers
Dies illa, that April, which brought May flowers.
Safer than the time before the baby
Crawls is the time before he smiles, maybe.
Stalin's merry moustache, magnetic, malignant,
Crawls slowly over a leaf which cannot move.

If the words sound queer and funny to your ear,
A little bit jumbled and jivey, it must be
Someone in 1943 you hear:
Who like a dog looking at a doorknob
Does not know why. Slats of daylight bob
On the wall softly, a gentle knocking, a breeze.
A caterpillar fills the bed which is
Covered with blood. 1943.
The stools in the toilet bowl, are they alive?

Harlem on fire rouged the uptown sky.
But the shot squeezed off in tears splashes short.
But bullets whizzing through hell need no alibi
Before they melt away. Intake. Compression,
Ignition, explosion. Expansion. Exhaust. Depression
Reddens the toilet paper. That black it feels.
Endomorphic round-fendered automobiles
Slow, startle each other, and bolt in herds across
Spuyten Duyvil for the Fifties and Westchester.

The cob stayed on the pond, perfect for Westchester,
Circling a nonexistent pen. Polly
Urethane sat on his face, Polly Esther
Sat on his penis. Protecting the non-cygnet.
Walking one day through the Piney Woods, he met
Three dogs in that peculiar light, strays. Two
Were shitting, looking off in that way dogs do,
Hunchbacked, sensitive, aloof, and neither
Male nor female. The third sat licking its teeth.

At the Institute they are singing *On Human*
Symbiosis and the Vicissitudes
of Individuation. Light of the One—
A summer sidewalk, a shadow shivered with leaves.
The mother smiles, *fa, so,* the mother grieves,
Beams down on the special bed for spinal
Injuries love that is primary and final,
Clear crystal a finger flicked that will ring a lifetime.
Plastic wrap refuse in the bare trees means spring.

And clouds blowing across empty sky.
A gay couple drags a shivering fist-sized
Dog down Broadway, their parachute brake. "Why
Robert Frost?" the wife one pleads, nearly
In tears; the other sniffs, "Because he
Believed in Nature and I believe in Nature."
Pacing his study past a book-lined blur,
A city dweller saw breasts, breast; their sour
And bitter smell is his own smoker's saliva.

The call had finally arrived from Perth:
He would live. C-4, a very high cervical
Lesion, but breathing on his own—rebirth
Into a new, another world, just seeing,
Without losing consciousness, and being,
Like being on the moon and seeing earth,
If you could breathe unaided. God, in Perth,
Twelve hours' time difference, thus day for night,
It was almost winter and almost Easter.

So accepting life is of the incredible.
2 a.m., the reeking silky monsoon
Air at Bombay Airport is edible,
Fertile, fecal, fetal—thunder—divine
Warm food for Krishna on which Krishna will dine.
The service personnel vacuum barefooted,
Surely Untouchables. Thunder. The booted
Back down the aisles spraying disinfectant,
By law, before disembarkation in Perth.

Down Under thunder thunder in formation
Delta wing Mach 2 dots time-warp to dust
Motes, climb and dissolve high above the one
Couple on the beach not looking up,
In the direction of Arabia, Europe,
Thunder, thunder, military jets,
Mars. The man smokes many cigarettes.
The man was saying to the woman, "Your son
Has simply been reborn," but can't be heard.

All is new behind their backs, or vast.
House lots link up like cells and become house,
Shade tree and lawn, the frontier hypoblast
Of capitalism develops streets in minutes
Like a Polaroid. The infinite's
Sublime indifference to the mile—Mao
On nuclear war. Inches; dust motes; they go bow wow
At the heels of history. The dust
Imitates the thunder that will bring rain.

By the Indian Ocean, he sat down
And wept. Snarl suck-suck-suck waaah. It was the Grand
Hôtel et de Milan. It was a gown
Of moonlight, moving, stirring a faint breeze,
Gauze curtains hissing softly like nylons please
Please crossing and uncrossing. Who—how had
The shutters opened? and the heavy brocade
Curtain? How far away the ceiling was.
The bedlamp. One floor below, Verdi died.

How far away Australia was, years.
A man asleep listened while his throat
Tried to cry for help. He almost hears
The brayed, longing, haunting whale song the deaf speak,
Almost words. Out of silence, sounds leak
Into silence, years. He lay there without
Love, in comfort, straining to do without,
And dreamed. A spaceship could reach the ceiling, the special
Theory of relativity says.

Leave love, comfort, not even masturbate,
Not even love justice, not even want to kill,
O to be sterile, and to rise and wait
On the ceiling at sunrise, for dawn! stainless blond
Ceiling, the beginning of the beyond!
But the TV showed outstretched hands—a revolver
Blocked the open door of the last chopper,
Struggling to get airborne. The ditto sheet served
With espresso began: *Good morning! Here are the news.*

Phosphorescent napkins don't make a bomb;
Under the parasols of Bicè's, via
Manzoni, chit-chat chased the firefly of Vietnam.
The courtyard flickered; the tablecloth glowed like lime.
Corrado Agusta's chow chow took its time
Turning its head to look at one, very
Refined and inhuman and dark as a mulberry,
Not a dog. Its blue tongue was not on view.
It had a mane and wore a harness, unsmiling.

Being walked and warmed up, they roared like lions on leashes.
The smell of castor oil. Snarl suck-suck-suck waaah
A racing motorcycle running through
The gears, on song; the ithyphallic faired
Shape of speed waaah an Italian's glans-bared
Rosso di competizione. The Counts
Agusta raced these Stradivarius grunts
As genteely as horse farms race horses—helicopter
Gunships, Agusta Aeronautiche.

The communists organized. Domenico
Agusta reigned. Of course the one who knew
Kennedys was the cold white rose Corrado.
The boss nailed each picket by name with a nod,
While Ciudad Trujillo and Riyadh
Kept unrolling more terror dollars for Corrado.
The iron and pious brother saw God go;
The salesman brother settled for everything:
Small arms fire, new nations; splits of brut, dry tears.

Domenico Agusta saw God go
Backwards like a helicopter in
A film he saw in Rome—i.e., in tow
With a helicopter. Sunbathers on Rome's
Roofs looked sideways from their cradled arms.
Just outside the window Jesus appears.
He faces us and steadily disappears.
The audience applauded. So odd to be
Agusta lifting off in your Agusta.

Goodbye. Goodbye. The stuck door was freed
And thrown open, and then closed and sealed.
The moviegoers of the world recede,
The White House and the tiny Marine band
Were wheeled away. A bulbously gloved hand
Frees the faulty door. Thrown open. Into
The countdown, and counting. -9. When you
Are no longer what you were. Thrown open.
-8. O let me out nor in.

Forty stories stock still like a boy
Whose height is being measured stands on smoke
As they withdraw the gantry, wheeled awoy,
Away. Perth Denpasar Djakarta Bangkok
Bombay in the capsule at the extreme tock,
La la, in the minute head above
The rest, eye movement peck peck like a dove,
A man sits on his back strapped down reading
Off numbers and getting younger, counting, cooing.

Millions of pounds of propellants make one dream,
Even more than psychoanalysis,
Of getting somewhere. Eyes glow in the gleam
Of the fuel gauges. Liquid oxygen
And kerosene. Check. Liquid oxygen
And liquid hydrogen—liquid in a freeze
Of −420°
F. Smoke boils off the ice that sheathes
The stainless steel building beneath him, forty floors.

Blue as the winder sapphire of the Cartier
Watch he has no use for now, goodbye,
The diodes of the digital display—
Information the color of his eyes,
As if his life were passing before his eyes,
−7. *Fin de race* face Louis
Cartier designed, inside a chewy
Candy of gold; face in a diver's helmet
Glassed in, prickles of the gold rivets and screws.

For everyday use, but by a Tutankhamen.
It would look feminine on a girl. The first
Wristwatch amused the sports of 1907.
The sport who commissioned the original,
The Brazilian Santos-Dumont, for a while
In 1906 believed he was the first man
To fly. Who says he did? None other than
The National Air and Space Museum says
Fernando Hippolyto da Costa does—

Believes Santos *was*. How could—but then
Who cares? Santos did not. Santos was not.
The watch was 1908, some say seven.
−6. What is there to believe in?
−6. What kind of god is not even
Immortal! −6. Nothing lasts.
A block of hieroglyphics trumpets, blasts
A golden long upended riff of silence,
It says for whom, whose name has been effaced.

To speak the name of the dead is to make them live
Again. O pilgrim, restore the breath of life
To him who has vanished. But the names they give.
No one can pronounce the hieroglyphs.
Then they had vowels to breathe with their bare midriffs,
Yes which? No one's known how to vocalize
The consonants. The kings don't recognize
Their names, don't recognize our names for them;
The soft parts that could not be embalmed are life.

One simply stares at the autistic face,
Charred rock-hard paper, a god. Stares at the stared-at.
Ramesses II in an exhibit case.
The Mummy Room is packed with Japanese
And German tours there to take in Ramesses.
The guides call in their languages, "This way please."
It seems one stares until one hardly sees.
It seems the room is empty. Like a dog
Looking at a doorknob, one stares at the stared-at.

As at a beetle rolling a ball of dung.
As at a large breast, with its nipple erect.
—5, soft and hard together among
The million things that go together one
Will lift away from, everything under the sun,
Everything—dog and doorknob—combustion to vapor
Lock—scissors cut paper, rock breaks scissors, paper
Covers rock. Everything is looking
For something softer than itself to eat.

Think of the energy required to get
Away from this hunt and peck for energy
That's running out. This need to look! O let
Your spirit rise above the engines below you.
Prepare for launch. O let a new way know you
Helmeted and on your back strapped down.
The moisture of the viscera, the blown
Coral rose of the brain on its stem—in this
Container, soft will never be exposed.

And leave behind the ancient recipes,
That cookbook for cannibals the Old Testament,
Bloody contemporary of course of Ramesses.
Cuisine minceur, urging one to eat less
But well. O Egypt! O Israel's salt sweetness!
From going soft and hard, from going up
And down, deliver us: struggling up
The steep path as Abraham with fire and knife,
And struggling down as Moses bent under the Law.

O let me go. O Israel! O Egypt!
The enemy's godless campfire at night, meat roasting
As you breathed near, sword drawn. *Cut.* Juice that dripped—
Later—from the dates from the hand of your daughter
Placed on your tongue in joy. Salute the slaughter.
O let me go. Salute the screenwriter,
DNA. Salute the freedom fighter
Kalishnikov machine pistol. A spider
Oiling the weapon spreads its legs and sighs.

TERROR OUR PLEASURE. O let me go. Logo
Of the age of ass—this age of movements—
Members and dismembers is our motto.
Oiling her weapon while in the mirror eyeing
Herself, turbaned in a black howli, sighing,
Is our muse *It feels good,* the spider. Mothers,
The children must die with dignity. Brothers,
Die. Mothers, calm the children. Squirt the poison
Far back in your child's throat. Stanza thirty-five.

Seated on your back strapped tight, tighter,
Feeling the contoured chair's formfitting
Love—no more hunt and peck on the typewriter
For energy that's running out. Stable
Fireproof love ideally comfortable!
You stare up at the gauges' radiance.
The mummy priest stares back in a trance,
And places beside you the silent clock radio,
And on the floor shoes for the long journey.

To lie on the horizon unable to rise—
How terrible to be the horizon! be
The expression in the quadriplegic's eyes,
Constant sunrise of feelings but no feeling.
The patient on the couch cow-eyes the ceiling.
Under his broken armor is a flower
Pinned down, that cannot reach its dagger, a flower.
Tongs in his skull, and dreams, not every man
Will wake. Can stand to look down at his penis and urine.

I am less than a man and less than a woman,
Wave after wave of moonlight breaks
On the trembling beach, dogs howl everywhere. One
Heave, and the water of the swimming pool
Sprang up, turning on its side like a pole-
Vaulter as it rose -4
In impossible slow motion. Whisper. Roar.
Because the stirred-up air only smells sweeter.
Because on Bali the earthquake toll is this sweet.

The Ketjak dancers roar and whisper *ketjak*
In ecstasy, the monkey dancers, k-*tchuck*.
They sway, but stay seated, *ketjak, ketjak*.
-3, C-4, we have ignition.
Lit up, the streets of Cairo are singing of urine,
The streets of Bombay are quiring human faeces.
-2 is the sea anemones
Which elsewhere are galaxies. Time-space is the amoeba's
Pouring motion into itself to move.

Organizations of gravity and light,
Supremely mass disappears and reappears
In an incomprehensible -1 of might.
Sat up at last, the quadriplegic boy
Feels beyond pain, feels beyond joy—
Still, stately as the Christ of Resurrection.
I wake beneath my hypnopompic erection,
Forty stanzas, forty Easters of life,
And smile, eyes full of tears, shaking with rage.

"Not to Be Born Is Obviously Best of All"

Your face swims to my window, beautiful
Translucence, a pearl, the fetal teardrop, little
Sea horse unswaying as time flows by. You nose
The glass, forever about to have a soul.
New York flows by, not now flows by, not now,
The traffic flows by. Moonlit dunes of amnesia
Flow by, flow by. In the rearview mirror dawn
The messenger sent back without a reply
Turning back into the Sahara.

O idea swimming on the blue,
Your face swims to the window, beautiful
Translucence against the blinding id of blue,
A leaf, the afterimage of a leaf,
Almost enough shade. I breathe in
Your breath and breathe a million miles away.
A mirror is backing through a blinding desert,
Autoroute to the end. Already there—
Still waiting! It is too late to be yourself.

To Robert Lowell and
Osip Mandelstam

I look out the window: spring is coming.
I look out the window: spring is here.
The shuffle and click of the slide projector
Changing slides takes longer.

I like the dandelion—
How it sticks to the business of briefly being.
Shuffle and click, shuffle and click—
Life, more life, more life.

The train that carried the sparkling crystal saxophone
Osip Mandelstam into exile clicketyclicked
Through suds of spring flowers,
Cool furrowed-earth smells, sunshine like freshly baked bread.

The earth was so black it looked wet,
So rich it had produced Mandelstam.
He was last seen alive
In 1938 at a transit camp near Vladivostok

Eating from a garbage pile,
When I was two, and Robert Lowell was twenty-one,
Who much later would translate Mandelstam,
And now has been dead two years himself.

I sometimes feel I hurry to them both,
Stand staring at the careworn spines
Of their books in my bookshelf,
Only in order to walk away.

The wish to live is as unintentional as love.
Of course the future always is,
Like someone just back from England
Stepping off a curb, I'll look the wrong way and be nothing.

Heartbeat, heartbeat, the heart stops—
But shuffle and click, it's spring!
The arterial branches disappearing in the leaves,
Swallowed like a tailor's chalk marks in the finished suit.

We are born.
We grow old until we're all the same age.
They are as young as Homer whom they loved.
They are writing a letter, not in a language I know.

I read: "It is one of those spring days with a sky
That makes it worthwhile being here.
The mailbox in which we'll mail this
Is slightly lighter than the sky."

Finals

A fat girl bows gravely like a samurai
On a bank of the Charles touching her toes,
Her tights in time with a sunrise sculler's stroke,
Then stroke, then stroke, dipped in pink, until
He crabs an oar, a burst of sudden white.

Four winters of grinding away then freaking on this
Soft-focus air not quite body temperature!
It feels pristine as the sweet-smelling world
Near a lawn sprinkler felt to a child.
Expulsion into Paradise for finals!

A red dome, and a green, a blue, a gold,
Veritas just above the leafiness.
The locked iron gates on Memorial Drive—
The eyes of a bachelor waiting for water to boil.

Men and Woman

Her name I may or may not have made up,
But not the memory,
Sandy Moon with her lion's mane astride
A powerful motorcycle waiting to roar away, blipping
The throttle, a roar, years before such a sight
Was a commonplace,
And women had won,

And before a helmet law, or
Wearing their hair long, had made all riders one
Sex till you looked again; not that her chest
Wasn't decisive—breasts of Ajanta, big blue-sky clouds
Of marble, springing free of her unhooked bra
Unreal as a butterfly-strewn sweet-smelling mountainside
Of opium poppies in bloom.

It was Union Square. I remember. Turn a corner
And in a light year
She'd have arrived
At the nearby inky, thinky offices of *Partisan Review*.
Was she off to see my rival Lief,
Boyfriend of girls and men, who cruised
In a Rolls convertible?

The car was the *caca* color a certain
Very grand envoy of Franco favored for daytime wear—
But one shouldn't mock the innocent machinery
Of life, nor the machines we treasure. For instance,
Motorcycles. What definition of beauty can exclude

The MV Agusta racing 500-3,
From the land of Donatello, with blatting megaphones?

To see Giacomo Agostini lay the MV over
Smoothly as a swan curves its neck down to feed,
At ninety miles an hour—entering a turn with Hailwood
On the Honda, wheel to wheel, a foot apart—
The tromboning furor of the exhaust notes as they
Downshifted, heard even in the photographs!
Heroes glittering on the summit before extinction

Of the air-cooled four-strokes in GP.
Agostini—Agusta! Hailwood—Honda!
I saw Agostini, in the Finnish Grand Prix at Imatra,
When Hailwood was already a legend who'd moved on
To cars. How small and pretty Ago was,
But heavily muscled like an acrobat. He smiled
And posed, enjoying his own charming looks,

While a jumpsuited mechanic pushed his silent
Racer out of the garage, and with a graceful
Sidesaddle run-and-bump started its engine.
A lion on a leash being walked in neutral
Back and forth to warm it up, it roared and roared;
Then was shut off, releasing a rather heady perfume
Of hot castor oil, as it docilely returned to the garage.

Before a race, how would Hailwood behave?
Racers get killed racing.

The roped-off crowd hushed outside the open door.
I stood in awe of Ago's ease—
In his leathers, like an animal in nature—
Inhumanly unintrospective, now smiling less
Brilliantly, but by far the brightest being in the room.

I feared finding his fear,
And looked for it,
And looked away so as not to mar the perfect.
There was an extraordinary girl there to study
Instead; and the altar piece, the lily
Painted the dried blood MV racing red,
Slender and pure—one hundred eighty miles an hour.

A lion which is a lily,
From the land of Donatello: where else could they design
Streamlined severe elegance in a toy color?
A phallus which was musical when it roared? By contrast,
Hailwood's Honda had been an unsteerable monster,
Only a genius could have won on it,
All engine and no art.

A lily that's a lion: handmade with love
By the largest helicopter manufacturer in Europe,
Whose troop carriers shielded junta and emir from harm,
And cicatriced presidents clutching
A golden ceremonial fly whisk and CIA dollars.
How storybook that a poor country boy
Should ride the Stradivarius of a Count—

The aristocrat industrialist Agusta—against
The middle-class son of a nicely well-off businessman;
English; and weekly wallowing near death
On the nearly ungovernable Japanese horsepower.
A clone of Detroit, Honda Company, in going for power,
Empire-building
In peacetime displaced to motorcycle sales.

Honda raced no more. No need to to
Sell Hondas now. The empire flourished elsewhere
Than glory. I swooned in the gray even indoor air
Of a garage in Finland, as racetime neared.
Daylight blinded the doorway—the day beyond,
The crowd outside, were far away. I studied
The amazing beauty, whom Ago seemed determined to ignore,

Seated like Agostini in skintight racing leathers.
Her suit looked sweet, like Dr. Denton's on a child;
Until—as she stood up—the infant's-wear blue-innocence
Swelled violently to express
The breasts and buttocks of a totem, Magna Mater,
Overwhelming and almost ridiculous,
Venus in a racing suit,

Built big as Juno—out of place but filling up
The room, if you looked at her, which no one else did;
Though I still couldn't tell

Who she was, whose friend she was, if she was anyone's;
Whose girl, the one woman in the room.
The meaning of the enormous quiet split
Into men and woman around the motorcycle.

I thought of Sandy Moon,
Advancing toward me through the years to find me there,
Moving toward me through the years across the room
I'd rented, to hide and work,
Near Foley Square; where I wrote, and didn't write—
Through the sky-filled tall windows
Staring out for hours

At the State Supreme Court building with its steps
And columns, and the Federal Courthouse with its,
And that implacably unadorned low solid, the Department
Of Motor Vehicles. I'd leaf
Through one of my old motorcycle mags
And think of Sandy Moon—and here she was,
Naked and without a word walking slowly toward me.

Women have won. The theme is
Only for a cello, is the lurking glow
Pooled in the folds of a rich velvet, darkly phosphorescent.
Summer thunder rumbled over Brooklyn, a far-off sadness.
Naked power and a mane of glory
Shall inherit the earth. Outside the garage,
The engine caught and roared—time to go.

Fucking

I wake because the phone is really ringing.
A singsong West Indian voice
In the dark, possibly a man's,
Blandly says, "Good morning, Mr. Seidel;
How are you feeling, God?"
And hangs up after my silence.

This is New York—
Some mornings five women call within a half hour.

In a restaurant, a woman I had just met, a Swede,
Three inches taller
Than I was among other things, and immensely
Impassive, cold,
Started to groan, very softly and husky voiced.
She said,
"You have utter control over me, and you know it.
I can't do anything about it."
I had been asking her about her job.

One can spend a lifetime trying to believe
These things.

I think of A.,
Before she became Lady Q.,
Of her lovely voice, and her lovely name.
What an extraordinary new one she took
With her marriage vows,

Even as titles go, extra fictitious. And ah—
And years later, at her request, paying a call on the husband
To ask if I could take her out
Once more, once, m'lord, for auld lang syne. She still wanted
To run away;
And had,
Our snowed-in week in the Chelsea
Years before.
How had her plane managed to land?

How will my plane manage to land?

How wilt thy plane manage to land?

Our room went out sledding for hours
And only returned when we slept,
Finally, with it still snowing, near dawn.

I can remember her sex,
And how the clitoris was set.

Now on to London where the play resumes—
The scene when I call on the husband. But first,

In Francis Bacon's queer after-hours club,
Which one went to after
An Old Compton Street Wheeler's lunch,
A gentleman at the bar, while Francis was off pissing,

Looking straight at me, shouted
"Champagne for the Norm'!"
Meaning normal, heterosexual.

The place where I stayed,
The genteel crowded gloom of Jimmy's place,
Was England—coiled in the bars of an electric fire
In Edith Grove.
Piece by piece Jimmy sold off the Georgian silver.
Three pretty working girls were his lodgers.

Walking out in one direction, you were in
Brick and brown oppidan Fulham.
Walking a few steps the other way, you heard
Augustus John's many mistresses
Twittering in the local Finch's,
And a few steps further on, in the smart restaurants,
The young grandees who still said "gels."

There was a man named Pericles Belleville,
There is a man named Pericles Belleville,
Half American.

At a very formal dinner party,
At which I met the woman I have loved the most
In my life, Belleville
Pulled out a sterling silver-plated revolver

And waved it around, pointing it at people, who smiled.
One didn't know if the thing could be fired.

That is the poem.

Pressed Duck

Caneton à la presse at the now extinct Café Chauveron.
Chauveron himself cooking, fussed
And approved
Behind Elaine, whose party it was;
Whose own restaurant would be famous soon.

Poised and hard, but dreaming and innocent—
Like the last Romanovs—spring buds at thirty, at thirty-two,
We were green as grapes,
A cluster of February birthdays,
All "Elaine's" regulars.

Donald, Elaine's then-partner,
His then-wife, a lovely girl; Johnny
Greco, Richardson, Elaine, my former wife, myself:
With one exception, born within a few days and years
Of one another.

Not too long before thirty had been old,
But we were young—still slender, with one exception,
Heads and necks delicate
As a sea horse,
Elegant and guileless

Above our English clothes
And Cartier watches, which ten years later shopgirls
And Bloomingdale's fairies would wear,
And the people who pronounce chic *chick*.
Chauveron cut

The wine-red meat off the carcasses.
His duck press was the only one in New York.
He stirred brandy into the blood
While we watched. Elaine said, "Why do we need anybody
 else?
We're the world."

What One Must Contend With

There was a man without ability.
He talked arrogance, secretly sick at heart.
Imagine law school with his terrible stutter!—
He gagged to be smooth. But it wasn't good.
Hadn't he always planned to move on to writing?
Which of course failed, how would it not? He called
Himself a writer but it didn't work,
He chose middling friends he could rise above
But it made no difference, with no ability.

He talked grand, the terrible endearing stutter.
Batting his eyes as if it felt lovely.
He batted and winced his self-hate, like near a sneeze.
He wrote and wrote, still he could not write,
He even published, but he could not write:
The stories one story of honey and abuse—
Love and the law—he was the boy . . . de Sade
Scratching his quill raw just once to get it off.
His pen leaked in *Redbook* the preseminal drool.

He must do something, do *something*. Boy you can
Reminisce forever about Harvard,
The motorboat won't run on your perfume,
Endless warm anecdotes about past girls
Aren't a wax your cross-country skis will ride on.
He took an office just like Norman Mailer.
He married a writer just like—yes exactly.
He shaved his beard off just like—et cetera.
It is a problem in America.

You never know who's dreaming about you.
They must do *something* to try to shift the weight
They wear—painted and smiling like gold the lead!
No wonder he walked staidly. They've time to dream.
Oh hypocrites in hell dying to catch up!
Oh in etterno faticoso manto!
And if you hail one and stop—he's coming—he'll stutter,
"Costui par vivo all'atto della gola,"
"This man seems alive, by the working of his throat."

The dreaming envying third-rate writhe in America.
He sucked his pipe. He skied he fished he published.
He fucked his wife's friends. Touching himself he murmured
He was not fit to touch his wife's hem.
He dreamed of running away with his sister-in-law!
Of doing a screenplay. Him the guest on a talk show—
Wonderful—who has read and vilifies Freud!
How he'd have liked to put Freud in his place,
So really clever Freud was, but he was lies.

It was autumn. It rained. *His* lies drooped down.
It was a Year of the Pig in Vietnam,
In Vietnam our year the nth, the Nixonth,
Sometimes one wants to cut oneself in two
At the neck. The smell. The gore. To kill! There was
The child batting her head against the wall,
Beating back and forth like a gaffed fish.
There was the wife who suspected they were nothing.
There's the head face-up in the glabrous slop.

You feel for him, the man was miserable.
It's mad t-*tooh*be so ad hominem!
And *avid,* when the fellow was in Vermont,
For Southeast Asia. Was he miserable?
Another creative couple in Vermont,
The wife toasts the husband's trip to New York,
The little evening he's planning. In less than a day
He will enter my poem. He picks at her daube.
There's the head face-up in the glabrous slop.

Voilà donc quelqu'un de bien quelconque!
Ah Vermont! The artists aggregate,
A suburb of the Iowa Writers' Workshop
Except no blacks with no ability.
I am looking down at you, at you and yours,
Your stories and friends, your banal ludicrous dreams,
Dear boy, the horror, mouth uncreating,
Horror, horror, I hear it, head chopped off,
The stuttering head face-up in a pile of slop.

Just stay down there dear boy it is your home.
The unsharpened knives stuck to the wall
Magnet-bar dully. The rain let off the hush
Of a kettle that doesn't sing. Each leaf was touched,
Each leaf drooped down, a dry palm and thin wrist.
His beautifully battered sweet schoolboy satchel walked
With him out the door into scrutiny,
The ears for eyes of a bat on the wings of a dove.
Art won't forgive life, no more than life will.

Homage to Cicero

Anything and everyone is life when two
Radios tune to the news on different stations while
A bass recorder pulses familiar sequences of sound waves,
An old sad sweet song, live. A computer
On stage listens to it all and does a print-out
Of it in Fortran, after a microsecond lag, and adds its own
Noise. The print-out piles up in folds
On the stage, in a not quite random way.
"Plaisir d'Amour" was the song.

Balls of cement shaped by a Vassar
Person, "majored in art at Vassar,"
Each must weigh a hundred pounds, fill a gallery.
They are enough alike to be perhaps
The look of what? The weight the person was
When she first was no longer a child—
Her planet lifeless after the Bomb—an anorexic image.
The hideous and ridiculous are obsessed
By the beautiful which they replace.

It is an age we may not survive.
The sciences know. We do believe in art
But ask the computer to hear and preserve our cry.
O computer, hear and preserve our cry.
Mortem mihi cur consciscerem
Causa non visa est, cur optarem multae causae.
Vetus est enim, "ubi non sis qui fueris,
Non esse cur velis vivere." Or, in English:
We are no longer what we were.

Descent into the Underworld

A woman watches the sunrise in her martini,
And drinks—and drinks darkness.
She is in a dark room,
Tubes in her nostrils and arms.

She is in her childhood bed.
Suddenly she is awake. Orpheus,
A big person, is about to do
Something to a little.

Floating in darkness, connected
To tubes like a diver . . . Eurydice.
Her breath-bubbles rise. Backing out of her throat
One by one, the Valiums rise.

Sweets to the sweet, yellow pills for a princess—
Orpheus holds out a bouquet
Of yellow tulips like a torch,
And shines it on her, and stares down at her.

She drinks his syrup, drooling in her sleep.
She lisps in a happy little girl's voice:
"The man is bad—I hate him.
The little girl is bad. She loves him."

A Beautiful Day Outside

I still lived, and sat there in the sun,
Too depressed to savor my melancholia.
I wore a cardboard crown. I held
A sceptre with a star on top.

I was on a hill, looking over at a mountain.
The sky was bald blue above.
Pine needles made
Something softer than a breast beneath the fits-all royal hose.

I was like an inmate of Charenton
Dully propped up on a throne outdoors, playing
"Fatigue of the Brave"—fatigue such as of a fireman holding
A still warm baby, waiting for the body bag.

Professional depression,
In an age of revolutionary fire
And having to grow up. This king did not wish to—
Still declined to be beheaded at forty-three.

But that I was depressed,
I had diagnosed the depression thus:
Ambivalence at a standstill—
Party-favor crown, real-life guillotine.

I still lived. I sat there in the sun:
Just water and salt conducting a weak current
Between the scent of pine and the foot smell
Of weeds reeking in the hot sun.

The children's party crown I wore
Dazzled my thinning hair like a halo.
The crown was crenellated like a castle wall.
A leper begged outside the wall.

In an upper gallery of the castle,
A young woman curtsied to the king and said: "Sire,
You are a beautiful day outside."
The king stuck his stick down her throat to shut her up.

Children, of all things bad, the best is to kill a king.
Next best: to kill yourself out of fear of death.
Next best: to grovel and beg. I took for my own motto
I rot before I ripen.

Years Have Passed

Seeing you again.
Your glide, your gaze.
Your very quiet voice.
Your terror. Your quiet eyes.

The Girl in the Mirror

Oh never to be yourself,
Never to let be
And simply be there.

The same
Morning ink blot in the mirror
Making a face up,

Making up a face. You need
All your strength
Never to be yourself.

Skirt, boots and sweater
Green as a stem.
I'll wear them.

Take me down from the shelf.
Oh never to be yourself
And always to be the same.

Like the air and the wind,
The wind and the air.
I hear a very quiet voice,

Emphatic like a flower,
Saying
It is I.

Fever

The soft street canyon was silent. In silence the new snow
Layered a rolling swell. The greatest evening
Tilted and rose against the tiny window:
Like her juggled soaking fishbowl swinging
A wave that burst into suds. A feeler of ice,
See-through and frail, scaled the whitening lace
Of the window guard, now more visible,
As if a vine were growing its own trellis.
The warm room watched it whiten, counting the minutes.

Think fast! (Still dreaming?) The boy had caught his friend
Flush with a lobbed cannonball of snow.
But then they crossed the closed street hand in hand.
Their dog sprinted in zigzags like a minnow,
Or wallowing in too deep, leapt out like a deer,
Folded forepaws leaping, then his rear.
From two floors up, two floors below is deep.
They don't know it, but sometime someone will come
And take her hand and feed her to the moon.

Erato

Suddenly the pace
Quickens, chill air dusts the air.
The leaves shrink
To a fawn color, held by their tails like mice,
The color of twine.

The fifty o'clock moon
Laid its cheek against the window,
Lay like snow on the carpet.
Outside the window,
Harlem in moonlight.

You walked outside.
Everyone knows
About the would-be suicide: you walk—
A step, a heartbeat—
Heartbeats. Sobsob, in the noon park,

The nannies were white,
Seated like napkins on the benches,
Starched and folded to sit up.
The babies did not choose the carriages,
Limousine coffers, blackly London;

They did not choose the rayless Tartar sun,
Sterile as the infected
Industrial steppes of Calvin—of
Bayonne. The reservoir banks were a purple socket
Like a black tulip.

Anything would do now
That inspired you
Below the Ninth Sphere, below the fixed stars
With fall, the electric cattle prod,
The cold juice that shocked you from your sleep

Lovelorn: slight,
Frizzy, sweating animal with feelings.
For fall, dawn rises in combers
Above the radiator shield's metal caning,
The sill flows like a pennant.

You smell the back-to-school,
Steam and rain on wool,
The tears not learning
And learning to write
With the sharp new chalk

Jacobean black and white,
The fantastic wrong and right, now dissolving
In Jamesian gray. You want to be a child—
You want to find the way
To either more or less than you are.

If you could choose.
Everywhere changes or fades.
Her hair streams like a willow's

As it leans to the river
When she leans toward you

Her anodyne, her healing face,
Eurasian, gypsy ease
(You have your memories),
Lovely lost love;
Erato's dark hair.

De Sade

So now you've fettered that sweet bride,
The boy you've toyed with a while and gelded,
And still not come, wretched sod.
Suck yourself off, like in your dream.

Innocents, white and fresh, bless 'em,
They belonged down in your love grotto;
They hiccup and honk on the slick flags
Looped with turds and the squashed-flat intestine.

Nothing helps, Marquis. Oh try
The scaffold again, with your bald pregnant nun.
The hired child caresses the ripped breasts;
She fingers herself, and releases the pretend-drop—

Nothing helps! At least, at least—
Sade save our republican Mistress, France.
Kiss the Courrèges boot, de Sade,
The stockingful up to the stocking top.

Beyond you lies the shrine, between
The slopes of Zion, past the alehouse.
Refresh yourself, drink deep. The brine!
The salt and gall, your honey and wine!

The New Frontier

Never again to wake up in the blond
Hush and gauze of that Hyannis sunrise.
Bliss was it
In that dawn to be alive

With our Kool as breakfast,
Make-do pioneers. Like politicians
Headed for a back room,
Each minute lived when it arrived,

And was the future. To be our age
Was very heaven. The fresh print
On the leaves dabbed
The windowscreen leaf-green;

A nestling's wing of a breeze that
Could not have stirred a cobweb
Eased through the air
And swept the room clean.

We could love politics for its mind!
All seemed possible,
Though it was barely a breeze.
The spirey steel-wool tuft in the map

Spreading apart, the city's
Wild wire and grease-rot,
Must be redeemed. When we returned
We would begin.

The city was our faith—
Ah we knew now the world need not end.
The flagpole out on the common actually
Seemed to tense,

Attentive as a compass needle,
Seemed caught in the open
Sniffing the breeze,
The little flag quivering like a sprig.

Alas. We could almost see
Cloth milk flying in place of blood and stars:
A nationless white flag colorlessly
Compounded of all colors, for peace.

But the pitcher and turned-down tumbler
On their doily summed up
The trim smell of dill,
We would begin.

It was new Eden.
And there was the young light,
There the feathery sapling—our tree priest,
Let us say, stuck with glued leaves.

Eden's one anthill bred
A commune honey pallor on the lawn

Uncurbed, yet innocent
Of any metaphor.

A pipe snaking around the baseboard rose
And stood silent in the corner like a birch.
Perhaps only innocence was keeping
The common still asleep

While we overreached, and touched so easily
What we were. We were
Awake while the world slept.
We overweened. Yes, yes,

We opened the patched screen
And plucked a leaf and stem,
And chewed the stem,
And tasted its green.

November 24, 1963

The trees breathe in like show dogs, stiffening
Under the silver leashes of light rain
To spines. A Cyclone fence that guards the moire
Embankment of the shrunken reservoir
Bristles with rain barbs, each a milk tooth, sting
Of stings, where fall began. The park's a stain,
The black paths shimmer under cellophane.

It is so real. Shy ghosts of taxis sniff
And worry in the empty park streets, lost
And misted lights, and down Fifth Avenue:
The flags soak at half-staff, bloodshed and blue;
Bloodletting stripes repeating their mute riff;
Gray stars, wet Union sky of stars, crisscrossed
With petrifying folds and sparks of frost.

The rain points prick the lake and touch the drought,
The dusk blue of a sterile needletip.
The brightness and the light has been struck down.

Freedom Bombs for Vietnam (1967)

The bald still head is filled with that grayish milk—
It's a dentist's glass door. It turns heavily—
There may be a weight in it. It weighs one ton.

Very even light diffuses through the globe.
But this surprise: life-squiggles, fishhooks,
Minnowhooks, surround the mineral eyes.

Someone like Muzak is burbling slant rhymes—
-*om* and -*am,* -*om* and -*am*—and holds up a telltale map
Of rice swimming in blood like white flies.

Ears almost as large as the President's
And more eloquent than lips,
That swallow toothlessly like polyps.

A spit glob and naked flashbulbs pop in Rusk's ear
And go down with whole heads, whole fields of heads
Of human hair, jagged necks attached.

Tangled unwashed bangs lengthening and cut, lengthening and
    cut,
The civilian population knows no more
Than a cellar of pocked Georgia potatoes.

This Press Talk is like a ham discussing pigs—
They need our help. He's a cracker showing the kids
The funny human shapes his potatoes have.

They must be scrubbed and eaten in their skins.
That's the nourishment. Rusk sets no other condition.
Rusk's private smile that looks like incest.

Robert Kennedy

I turn from Yeats to sleep, and dream of Robert Kennedy,
Assassinated ten years ago tomorrow.
Ten years ago he was alive—
Asleep and dreaming at this hour, dreaming
His wish-fulfilling dreams.
He reaches from the grave.

Shirtsleeves rolled up, a boy's brown hair, ice eyes
Softened by the suffering of others, and doomed;
Younger brother of a murdered president,
Senator and candidate for president;
Shy, compassionate and fierce
Like a figure out of Yeats;
The only politician I have loved says *You're dreaming* and says
The gun is mightier than the word.

The Drill

"Have the bristles at an angle and gently
  Work them in between the tooth and gum
  Back and forth," a woman says.
  Her breast is next to my ear.
  She moves a set of teeth four inches high
  And a foot-long toothbrush.

  Breast; and then the teeth; and then
  The window without a shade or curtains—then the day,
  Twelve floors above the street;
  And the empty lighted office windows always
  On the other side of a street
  From the drill,
  Since childhood,
  The obsolete slow drill that now only polishes.

Hamlet

Alive. Yes and awake. Flowers
Fall through his mind, in one slant, like snow.
The electric toothbrush flames in his hand.
Mozart sweetens the small room.

LSD tears he wept all night,
One hundred for a dead father.
LSD tears, they roll heavy
And burn like molten metal drops.

Now as the drug wears off he waits.
For a mother has remarried.
Oh the man swelled, supple bitch,
And smiled as if he might give birth.

Completely to be shut of both,
Purged pure and bare to all in one's fate,
The drug makes possible at last
[*The curtain stirs*], out of the shell,

The old self, new and neat as a chick.
This dew, haze softness on waking has opened
His window on the street a crack.
Midnight tolls. The curtain stirs.

The Future

Fifth Avenue has the flickers, heat
Lightning lit. A voodoo doll's
Whey little bursts of breath stare,
And fits of fluttering like an eye;

A Haitian nurse at her window altar
Tutoyers the hatpin. The terrified trees'
Bursts of breath stare, as though Fifth
Were lined with dandelion clocks.

Scree in the void, Sinai is snuffed,
Half recreated. Parting the black:
Arrow one-way signs plunged through,
The twitched buildings dancing and chalk-white.

It is too late for people but
A rag barfs on a curb. But it's
A sandwich board mouldering there
Draws the nose of his tetchy chow:

Seen in a sheet-flap of sight just now
And gone now. In the blinded dark;
Streetlights, stars sapped—repeated blows
That leave unstirred the humid silence.

Silence . . . Even Harlem is still—
Harlem is near. The galaxies,
The brainstorms of zero, gasp the fainter
And fainter last breaths of the future.

This time we may go out for good.
Blacked out after the zillionth stroke.
This may be a good time not to wake.
Fifth Ave. The white man's night-light, the future.

Wanting to Live in Harlem

Pictures of violins in the Wurlitzer collection
Were my bedroom's one decoration,
Besides a blue horse and childish tan maiden by Gauguin—
Backs, bellies and scrolls,
Stradivarius, Guarnerius, Amati,
Colored like a calabash-and-meerschaum pipe bowl's
Warmed, matured body—

The color of the young light-skinned colored girl we had then.
I used to dream about her often,
In sheets she'd have to change the day after.
I was thirteen, had just been bar mitzvah.
My hero, once I'd read about him,
Was the Emperor Hadrian; my villain, Bar Kokhba,
The Jew Hadrian had crushed out at Jerusalem:

Both in the *Cambridge Ancient History*'s Hadrian chapter (1936
Edition), by some German. (The Olympics
Year of my birth and Jesse Owens' *putsch* it had appeared.)
Even then, in '49, my mother was dying.
Dressed in her fresh-air blue starched uniform,
The maid would come from mother's room crying
With my mother's tears shining on her arm,

And run to grab her beads and crucifix and missal,
I to find my violin and tuning whistle
To practice my lessons. Mendelssohn. Or Bach,
Whose Lutheran fingering had helped pluck
The tonsured monks like toadstools from their lawns,

And now riddled the armor I would have to shuck:
His were life-sized hands behind his puppet Mendelssohn's.

One night, by the blue of her nitelite, I watched the maid
Weaving before her mirror in the dark, naked.
Her eyes rolled, whiskey-bright; the glass was black, dead.
"Will you come true? It's me, it's me," she said.
Her hands and her hips clung to her rolling pelvis.
Her lips smacked and I saw her smile, pure lead
And silver, like a child, and shape a kiss.

All night I tossed. I saw the face,
The shoulders and the slight breasts—but a boy's face,
A soft thing tangled, singing, in his arms,
Singing and foaming, while his blinding pelvis,
Scooped out, streamed. His white eyes dreamed,
While the black face pounded with syncope and madness.
And then, in clear soprano, we both screamed.

What a world of mirrored darkness! Agonized, elated,
Again years later I would see it with my naked
Eye—see Harlem: doped up and heartless,
Loved up by heroin, running out of veins
And out of money and out of arms to hold it—where
I saw dead saplings wired to stakes in lanes
Of ice, like hair out cold in hair straightener.

And that wintry morning, trudging through Harlem
Looking for furnished rooms, I heard the solemn

Pedal-toned bowing of the Bach Chaconne.
I'd played it once! How many tears
Had shined on mother's maids since then?
Ten years! I had been trying to find a room ten years,
It seemed that day, and been turned down again and again.

No violin could thaw
The rickety and raw
Purple window I shivered below, stamping my shoes.
Two boys in galoshes came goose-stepping down
The sheer-ice long white center line of Lenox Avenue.
A blue-stormcoated Negro patrolman,
With a yellowing badge star, bawled at them. I left too.

I had given up violin and left St. Louis,
I had given up being Jewish,
To be at Harvard just another
Greek nose in street clothes in Harvard Yard.
Mother went on half dying.
I wanted to live in Harlem. I was almost unarmored . . .
Almost alone—like Hadrian crying

As his death came on, "Your Hadrianus
Misses you, Antinous,
Misses your ankles slender as your wrists,
Dear child. We want to be alone.
His back was the city gates of Rome.
And now Jerusalem is dust in the sun,
His skies are blue. He's coming, child, I come."

The Last Entries
in Mayakovsky's Notebook

She loves me? She loves me not?

I wring
My hands and scatter the broken-off fingers.
Like petals you pluck from some
White little flower along your way.
You hold them up to the breeze,
They've told your fortune,
They drift off into May.

Though
Now a haircut
Lays bare thorns of gray,
Though my morning shave shows me
On the bib the salt of age,
I hope, I believe

I will never weaken.

Never be caught
Showing good sense.

•

Past one o'clock. You must have gone to sleep.
Or do

You feel, perhaps you feel the same as I?
I'm in no hurry.

Is
There no point

In a telegram that would only
Wake you? And disturb you.

.

The tide ebbs.
The sea too
Is going to sleep.
The incident as they say
Is closed.
Love's skiff
Has stove
In on the daily grind.
It would be useless
Making a list
Of who did what to whom.
We shared
Weapons
And wounds.

.

Past one. Like a

Silent moonlit Oka', the Milky Way
Streams into the night. I'm in no hurry.

As they say: the incident is closed.
A telegram would wake you.

How still it is.
Night, night sky, and stars.

What stillness there is in the world!
What stillness we are capable of!

In hours like these one rises
To address the Ages—History—the Universe!

•

I know
The power of words.

(Not the gas
The loges applaud.)

That make
Coffins rear up and break loose

And clomp off
Robotlike, rocked forward like a crate.

So we are rejected,
So we go unpublished

But the word gallops on, cinching the saddle tighter,
The word rings for centuries—a tocsin!

And steam engines creep up to lick
Poetry's calloused hands.

I know
The power of words.

It is nothing!
A fallen

Petal under
A dancer's heel.

But man
In his soul, his lips, in his bones . . .

Hart Crane Near the End

1

The woman in love with him
Pleads with him, "Why
Must there be such misery?
What is there in you that wants this?"
And still he does not feel it,
Feels nothing, sealed in his self.

The beach house is filled up.
The guests drift in and out
Talking in wafts, sozzled,
Sunburns moonlit; dappled fluttering
Shirts at summery games. But
Now near dawn it's cold. He sees
The clock ticks swimming through the air,
Swimming eyelashed eyelets tiny as rotifers.
A warped smile is everywhere,
Half in, half out of water.

In youth more delicate than the boy Rimbaud's,
The sunset nose, lips like blood sausages.
Course of the day's
Lost, unsought breaths, uncounted,
Each separate as a life, a guest.
His life had purposes!
The hall clock ticks.
Oh the heresies, Oh each distinct,
Blue and bright and trite and evil, each,

Those efforts to see the light
Chasing each other's tails—
Whirled into moral butter like Black Sambo's tigers,
As the phonograph spins Ravel's "Bolero."

2

A glance—a snipe's beak—
Opens, he sees
The scorched
Tobacco-y nerve ends.
They are wandering through the sumac,
Wondering if it is poisonous,
Blondes and brunettes.
"Who belongs to you?" she whispers.

His life is falling.
His butched unruly hair boils
Through her fingers like the ocean.
The sun beats lightning on the waves,
The waves fold thunder on the sand.
She is afraid.

3

Raising his cigar and drink,
He gives a toast: "To the dying
Wildlife of Mexico—myself!
Ah, to Lorenzo,
Of course, too.

At forty-five, at his noon eclipsed—
Our former neighbor, up there
In heaven with Beiderbecke.
The famous style was just the life,
He handed you the books blade-first,
Keen as a castaway's thirst.
His spirit,
Like a little straight stick,
A little straight stick,
So set and separate, so free,
Wrestled verse by verse
Favorite flowers, birds and beasts."

He barely finishes.
With a roar the surf razes
Last night's sand castle
And seizes her sailor's cap
As she gasps for breath,
Fighting back tears.
The white dot wags on the water
Like candlelight in a draft,
Flickers, dips and reappears—
As if, someone says, on an altar offered to
The anchored white United Fruit ship,
A hospital ship,
Which it seems to want to draw near.

"Why, it reverences United Fruit"
(Up goes his glass),

"Our brilliantined
  Hustler queen, our Muse.
  But our Muse keeps his pitch to himself now,
  From me anyway—that white lie,
  Inspirer of my verse, my
  Sermon on San Juan hill *The Bridge,*
  That hemorrhaged,
  Flowing out under the Morgan boardroom doors
  Like a ray stalking, a gliding
  Opera cape of blood.

"Sweetheart, don't cry. Let's see.
  Tolstoy is like the sea.
  Shakespeare is like the sea. Or let's say
  Whitman is like a spar
  Off the *America,*
  Wooed by the *Pequod,* the *Patna,* the *Lusitania,*
  The *Titanic,* the maniacs,
  The siren idealists—America
  Weltering in her element
  Like ambergris. Slick sightless mass,
  Clung to by a sweet smell.
  The old fag as he drowns still acting
  The little girl
  Who can come to no harm."

He still has his charm.
Her childless troubled soul quiets,
Glows like a flame in Vermeer;

Her startled little vices
Twinkle off like swallows.

"Don't cry, sweetheart.
Keep my kisses in your pocket
Till I get back. Oh, wouldn't you like to see
Ohio with me
On my trip!
But if I come back,
Who will put up with me?
Who will put me up?
Sunshine, I've no place to go,
And no place to go
Is easy enough to find."

4

On the desk
The paper is blank,
Freezing to sleep
In the snowfield cast by the lamp.
He tries to think;
Tries to remember the evening.
Faceless
Spondee and iamb couples kick by
In a conga line.
The baker, the breadline,
The Communist and Capitalist,

To them poetry is
A saint's temptation
And his desert, both.
The wide dry heartland sky,
The teetotaling Sahara
Over Chagrin Falls,
When he was last there,
Ideally white as Moby Dick,
Devoured him like a drop.

5

From the bed,
Through her jiggling cigarette
She recites: "Then you downed
The other bottle of tequila.
You said you were Baudelaire—
Or was it Marlowe?—
You said you were Blake
Talking English with the angels,
And said you were Christ, of course,
But *never* would say
You were yourself. And the voice!
The steady inhuman horror
Making my heart contract!
You cursed me, my makeup,
Cursed the moon, its light,
Cursed that boyfriend,
All your other friends, all the guests.

My God, you cursed the elements!
And separately, by name,
The heliotrope, the heaven-tree,
The star jessamine, the sweet-by-night;
And even the spring pool
With the small ducks, the lily pad;
And even the air we breathed together,
Because I breathed it and the flowers.
You wept. You said,
'There *is* goodness,
That from bayberry made modest candles
And rose jam from hips and haws.
And Blake talked English with the angels.'
And you wanted to make love to me,
Though I can't imagine how."

6

When morning breaks, he takes
His first drink of water in a day.
Petite veille d'ivresse, sainte!
His orange fireball eye sees,
Dried yolk yellow like a slicker,
The faded fire hydrant
Pop from the grass like a bird's note,
And its black beak tweets
Me! Me!

A selection of books published by Penguin is listed on the following pages.

For a complete list of books available from Penguin in the United States, write to Dept. DG, Penguin Books, 299 Murray Hill Parkway, East Rutherford, New Jersey 07073.

For a complete list of books available from Penguin in Canada, write to Penguin Books Canada Limited, 2801 John Street, Markham, Ontario L3R 1B4.

If you live in the British Isles, write to Dept. EP, Penguin Books Ltd, Harmondsworth, Middlesex.

SOME PENGUIN MODERN POETRY

A CALL IN THE MIDST OF THE CROWD
Alfred Corn

NEW AND SELECTED POEMS
Irving Feldman

LIFE AMONG OTHERS
Daniel Halpern

THE RETRIEVAL SYSTEM
Maxine Kumin

LIKE WINGS
Philip Schultz

SOME PENGUIN POETRY

WILLIAM BLAKE: THE COMPLETE POEMS
Edited by Alicia Ostriker

BROWNING: A SELECTION
Edited by W. E. Williams

BURNS: SELECTED POEMS
Edited by William Beattie and Henry W. Meikle

CONTEMPORARY AMERICAN POETRY
Edited by Donald Hall

DONNE: THE COMPLETE ENGLISH POEMS
Edited by A. J. Smith

ENGLISH AND AMERICAN SURREALIST POETRY
Edited by Edward B. Germain

GERARD MANLEY HOPKINS: POEMS AND PROSE
Edited by W. H. Gardner

BEN JONSON: THE COMPLETE ENGLISH POEMS
Edited by George Parfitt

JOHN KEATS: THE COMPLETE POEMS
Edited by John Barnard

MALLARMÉ: THE POEMS
Translated by Keith Bosley

ANDREW MARVELL: THE COMPLETE POEMS
Edited by Elizabeth Story Donno

THE METAPHYSICAL POETS
Edited by Helen Gardner

THE PENGUIN BOOK OF BALLADS
Edited by Geoffrey Grigson

V. S. Naipaul

A HOUSE FOR MR. BISWAS

As Mohun Biswas moves from job to job, acquiring a wife and four children, the odds against him lengthen and his ambition becomes more remote.

THE MYSTIC MASSEUR

Ganesh, who cured the Woman Who Couldn't Eat and the Man Who Made Love to His Bicycle, becomes involved in a local scandal. But he manages to keep some surprises in reserve. . . .

THE SUFFRAGE OF ELVIRA

"I promising you," said Mrs. Baksh of the Elvira district election in Trinidad, "for all it began sweet sweet, it going to end damn sour." And she was right. . . .

Also:

IN A FREE STATE
THE LOSS OF EL DORADO
MIGUEL STREET
THE MIMIC MEN
MR. STONE AND THE KNIGHTS COMPANION

Saul Bellow

HENDERSON THE RAIN KING

In this sparkling novel Nobel Laureate Saul Bellow recounts the adventures of Eugene Henderson, a prodigious American millionaire, in darkest Africa. Henderson "is a picaresque hero in the great tradition, full of bizarre vitality, with affinities both to Odysseus and to Don Quixote" —*Newsweek.*

HERZOG

Herzog tells the story of Moses Herzog, sufferer, joker, cuckold, charmer, and survivor of disasters both public and private. First published in 1964, it won the acclaim of critics and readers alike; it was a longtime best-seller, a selection of the Literary Guild, and a winner of the National Book Award for fiction and of the International Publishers' Prize.

MR. SAMMLER'S PLANET

A wry old man, once a resident of Krakow, of London, and of a Nazi death camp, strides recklessly through New York City's Upper West Side and through the pages of this extraordinary novel. Observing everything, appalled by nothing, Mr. Sammler notes with the same disinterested curiosity the activities of a pickpocket, the details of his niece's sex life, the madness of his own daughter, and the lunar theories of a Hindu scientist.

Also:

MOSBY'S MEMOIRS AND OTHER STORIES
SEIZE THE DAY

PORTABLE POETS OF THE ENGLISH LANGUAGE

Edited by W. H. Auden and Norman Holmes Pearson

Horace Gregory writes of this series: "I find it hard to use anything but superlatives on the Auden-Pearson collection of British and American verse. It is the best (and I know it is the best) comprehensive collection of its kind in existence. With Auden's introductions . . . it clearly shows what intelligent twentieth-century editing can do if enough brilliance and poetic insight go into it."

Volume I
MEDIEVAL AND RENAISSANCE POETS:
LANGLAND TO SPENSER

Volume II
ELIZABETHAN AND JACOBEAN POETS:
MARLOWE TO MARVELL

VOLUME III
RESTORATION AND AUGUSTAN POETS:
MILTON TO GOLDSMITH

Volume IV
ROMANTIC POETS: BLAKE TO POE

Volume V
VICTORIAN AND EDWARDIAN POETS: TENNYSON TO YEATS